the **BAD GUYS**

in

THEY'RE
BEE-HIND YOU!

AARON BLABEY

# the BAD GUYS

in

THEY'RE BEE-HIND YOU!

SCHOLASTIC INC.

Hey, look!
It's that dirty snake!
Let's get him!

Sure.

How about this—
I'll play the

**VENOMOUS SNAKE . . .**

Give it time,
little buddy.

*Give it time . . .*

# · CHAPTER 1 ·
# UNDERLORDS IN DISGRACE

YOU SOUND LIKE THE SNAKE.
"OOH, I DON'T KNOW HOW SHE DID IT. OOOH DEAR!"
I GIVE YOU CHAIN SAW HANDS AND YOU REPAY ME WITH WHIMPERS!

Listen, man, I was getting

through to Wolf. I really was.

He was **TURNING!**

But then Fox . . . she, like . . .

# EXPLODED.

She's *really* powerful.

I thought calling her **THE ONE** seemed

a bit over the top, but I gotta tell you—

SHE'S NOT POWERFUL!
THE MOMENT SHE DEFEATED YOU MAGGOTS, CARRIED TO THE NEXT UNIVERSE.
THE ONLY PROBLEM IS,

Dude, that's harsh. I realize I've *technically* failed twice now. And chain saw guy . . .

UNDERLORD SHAÅRD.

Sorry, Underlord Try Haåard . . . He didn't do any better than me.

I have to admit it, man . . .

WE NEED SOME HELP.

SCHOOOOOM!

I WILL DESTROY THEM ALL!

**GASP! HE'LL DESTROY THEM ALL!**

WHA . . . ?
What was that?!
I thought I heard . . .

Was that . . . *Piranha?*

SERPENT!

Remind me . . . what did I wish for again?

YOU ASKED FOR HELP.

AND HERE SHE IS...

*YOUR PRECIOUS FRIENDS ARE IN* **MY WORLD** *NOW.*

*LET'S GO AND PLAAAAY WITH THEM . . .*

They've been gone a while. How do you know they're *still in your world?*

Oh, darling.

I'm absolutely confident they'll

# STICK AROUND

in mine.

HAHAHAHAH

# CHAPTER 2

# GET IT?

What IS this?!
The ground is *sticky*.

SQUELCH!

. . . it's honey.

*HONEY?!*
I thought this was a
**BUILDING!**
Like, a BIG building.
Why would a building
be made of HONEY?
That doesn't make
any sense . . .

It's a
**NEW UNIVERSE.**
Anything is possible.

But who would make a
skyscraper out of honey?

*Who would do that?*

SQUELCH!

Fox?
*Can you
hear me?*

She's still out.

I say we head for the
**NEXT
DOORWAY.**

If her evil **HEAVY-METAL CENTIPEDE-LOOKING SUPERVILLAIN** is here, something tells me he'll find us.

If he's not, we'll just pass on through the next doorway. Agreed?

Sure.

Piranha said the next doorway is in **THE BASEMENT.**

Should we get him back into **ORACLE MODE** to check?

Again, with the honey? Seriously, get it off your chest— *WHO would build with honey?*

Bees!

Bees?

Bees.

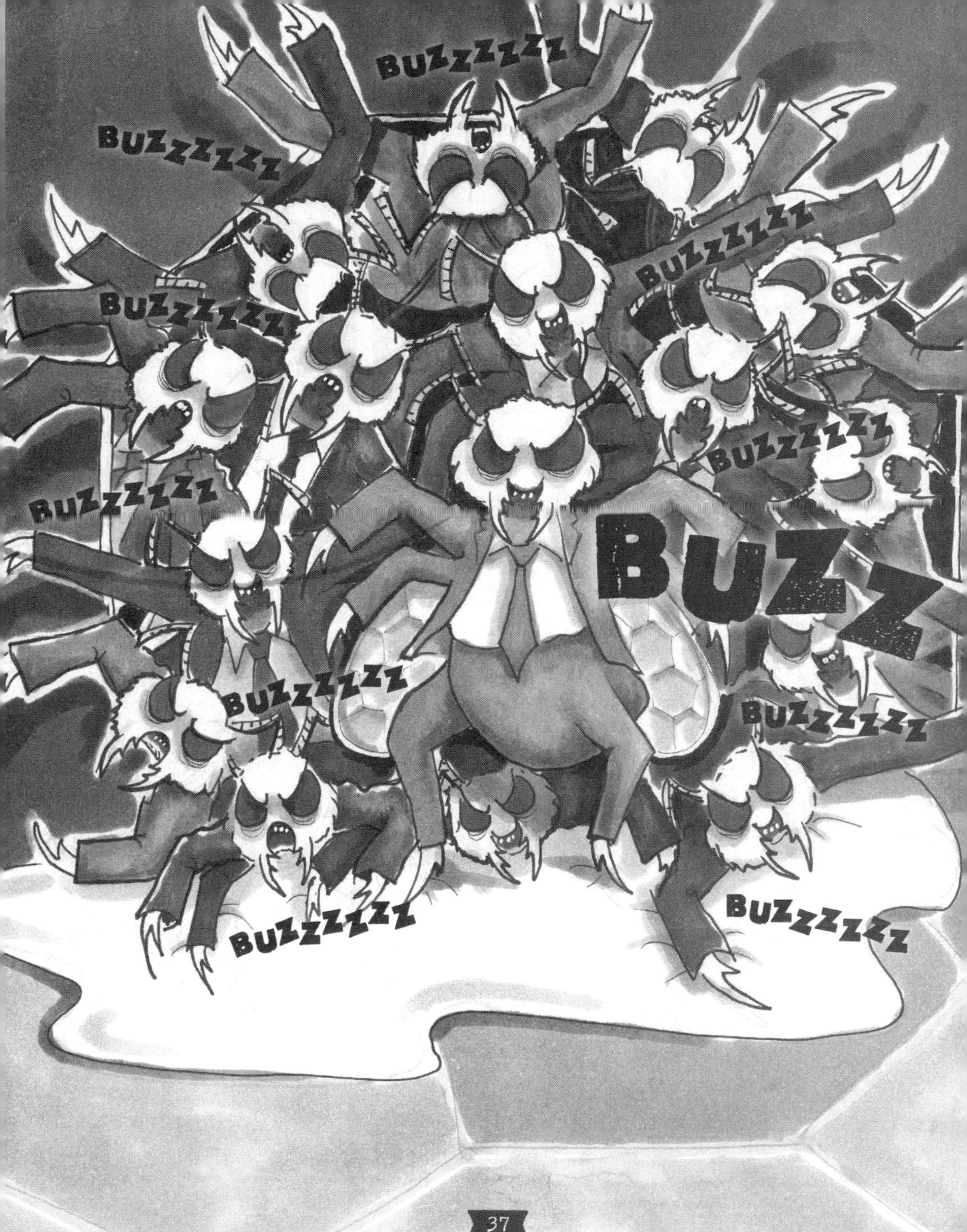

# CHAPTER 3

# HEY, IT'S A PARTY LINE!

**SEE!**
They're officially calling us
**THE B-TEAM!** I knew it!

NOT FOR LONG.
DO I LOOK LIKE I
BELONG ON THE
**B-TEAM?!**

No, you do not . . .

THE **B-TEAM**
IS IN **DANGER!**

Well, I **LOVE** danger.
What kind of danger?

**SUDDENLY, VERY, VERY, VERY, VERY FAR AWAY . . .**

HUH?!

There he is again!
I can hear . . .
PIRANHA?
And is that . . .
his dad?!

Underlord *WHO?!*

UNDERLORD SHAÅRD WILL DESTROY YOU.

UNDERLORD SHAÅRD WILL DESTROY US.

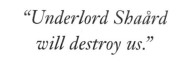

*"Underlord Shaård will destroy us."* Hmmm, I'm trying to put a positive spin on that sentence, but my mind's a blank . . .

That was weird, right?
Hands up if you thought
that was *weird*.

*WHAT?!*
What's weird?!
What just happened?
And what IS that smell?!
*WHAT IS GOING ON?!*

Hmmm.
What I have to say
might come as a
bit of a shock . . .

# · CHAPTER 4 ·
# HIVE FIGHT!

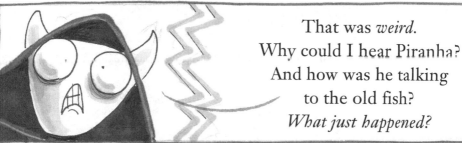

That was *weird*.
Why could I hear Piranha?
And how was he talking
to the old fish?
*What just happened?*

*Shush, darling!
Look! We've arrived!*

HA!

FAAAART!

SPLAT!

Snap out of it, buddy!

*That smell!
That terrible,
phantom smell!*

*GO ON, DARLINGS. GO INSIDE . . .*

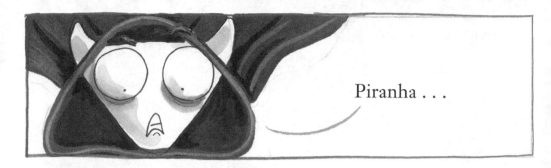

Piranha . . .

Are you ready, pal?
We need you.

Need me?
For what?

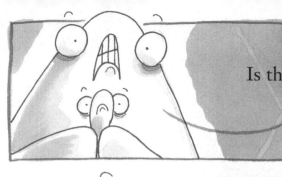

Is that his **STINGER?!**
Did he just break off
his own stinger?

I thought bees died
when their stingers
came off?

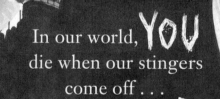

In our world, YOU
die when our stingers
come off . . .

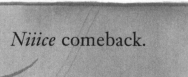

*Niiice* comeback.

Yeah. Wow.
That was *good*.

Hey, I'll . . .
I'll be back
in a minute . . .

*WHERE ARE YOU
GOING, DARLING?
YOU'LL MISS ALL
THE FUN!*

# · CHAPTER 5 ·
# PAPA ON THE MENU

I said
*WHAT?!*

Well . . .

You had a **VISION,**
Papa Piranha!

You said . . .

# UNDERLORD SHAÅRD IS COMING

and the only thing
that can save us is if . . .

If . . .

If what?

**THE DINOSAUR EATS YOU.**

Don't look at me like that.
YOU said it.

Wait—who is

**UNDERLORD SHAÅRD?**

We don't know.
But apparently he
wants to stop us from
finding THE OTHERS.

And who are

**THE OTHERS**
again?

We don't know.

And who is
**THIS GUY**
again?

*WE DON'T KNOW!*

*Then WHY should I listen to any of you?!*

Um, excuse me . . .

WHAT?!

STILL ON THE WRONG TEAM

GULP!

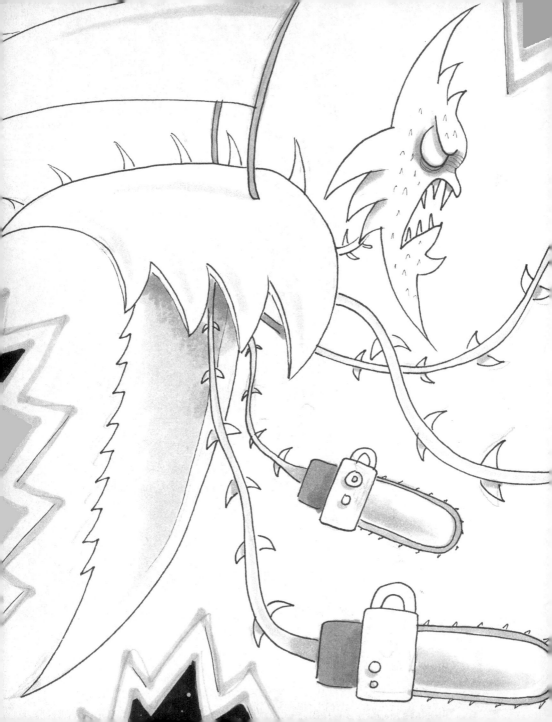

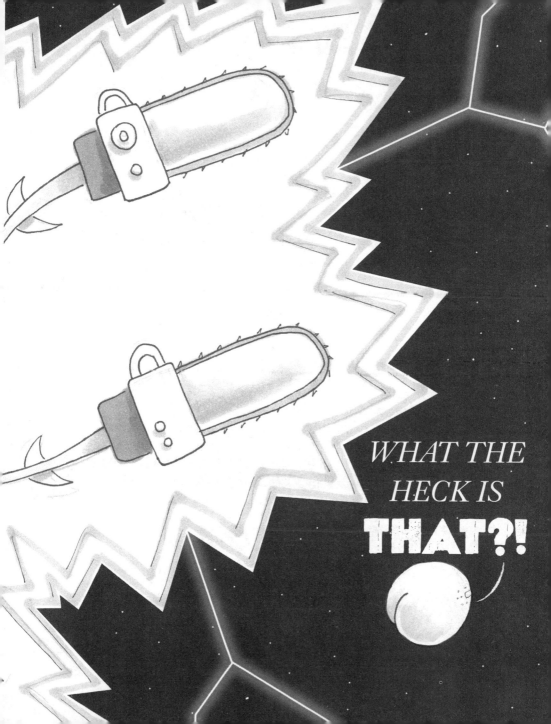

DANG! Full throttle! Let's hightail it outta here!

VRRRRR!

BLAAARRRTTTT!

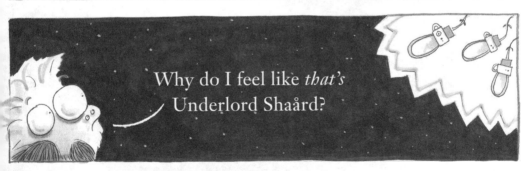

Why do I feel like *that's* Underlord Shaård?

MILTON!

STILL ON THE WRONG

Yes, let's think
this through for
a minute . . .

Jerky. Just think of him as *jerky*.

Papa?

I don't know why . . .
but something tells
me this is the
**RIGHT THING
TO DO.**

I can *feel* it.

Can you feel it, too?

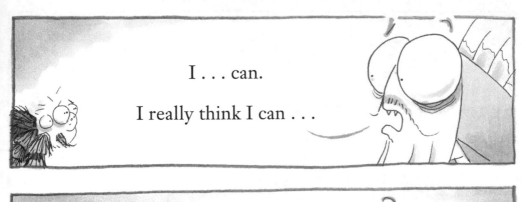

I . . . can.

I really think I can . . .

Can *you* feel it, my friend?

Umm . . .

Never mind, don't answer that . . .

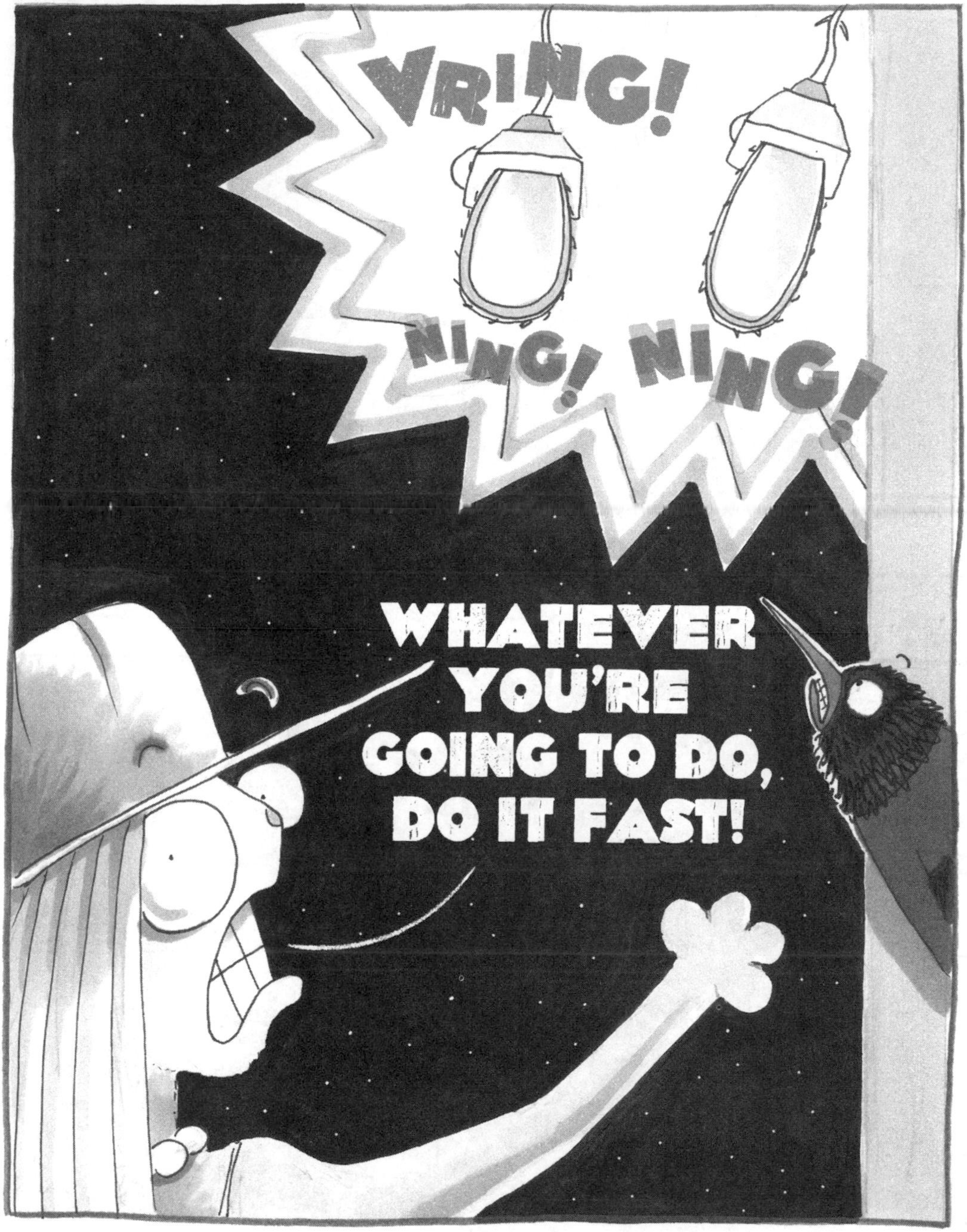

VRING!
NING! NING!
WHATEVER YOU'RE GOING TO DO, DO IT FAST!

Swallow me whole,
*dinosaurio.*
No choppers, OK?

Ready?

Umm . . .

EAT HIM RIGHT NOW!

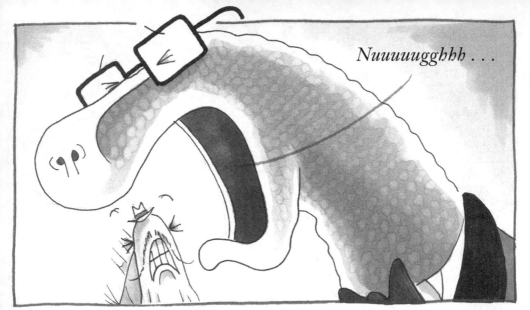

*Nuuuuugghhh . . .*

GULP!

Milton?
*Say something . . .*

But we *have* to get Fox to the next doorway . . .

Honey, we can't *find* those doorways without Pepe!

That's right! We can't do it *without* Piranha!

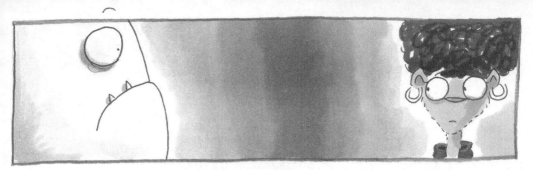

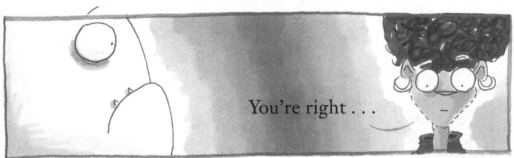

You're right . . .

WE HAVE TO **SPLIT UP.**

LAST WARNING. PUT DOWN YOUR WEAPONS.

But . . .

Two things—

What?

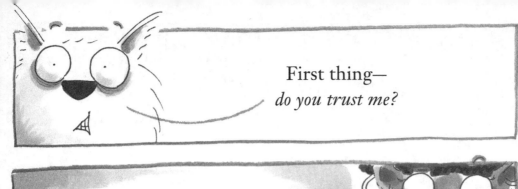

First thing—
*do you trust me?*

Yeah.
I do.

But what's the second thing?

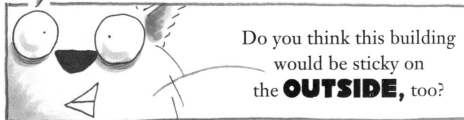

Do you think this building
would be sticky on
the **OUTSIDE,** too?

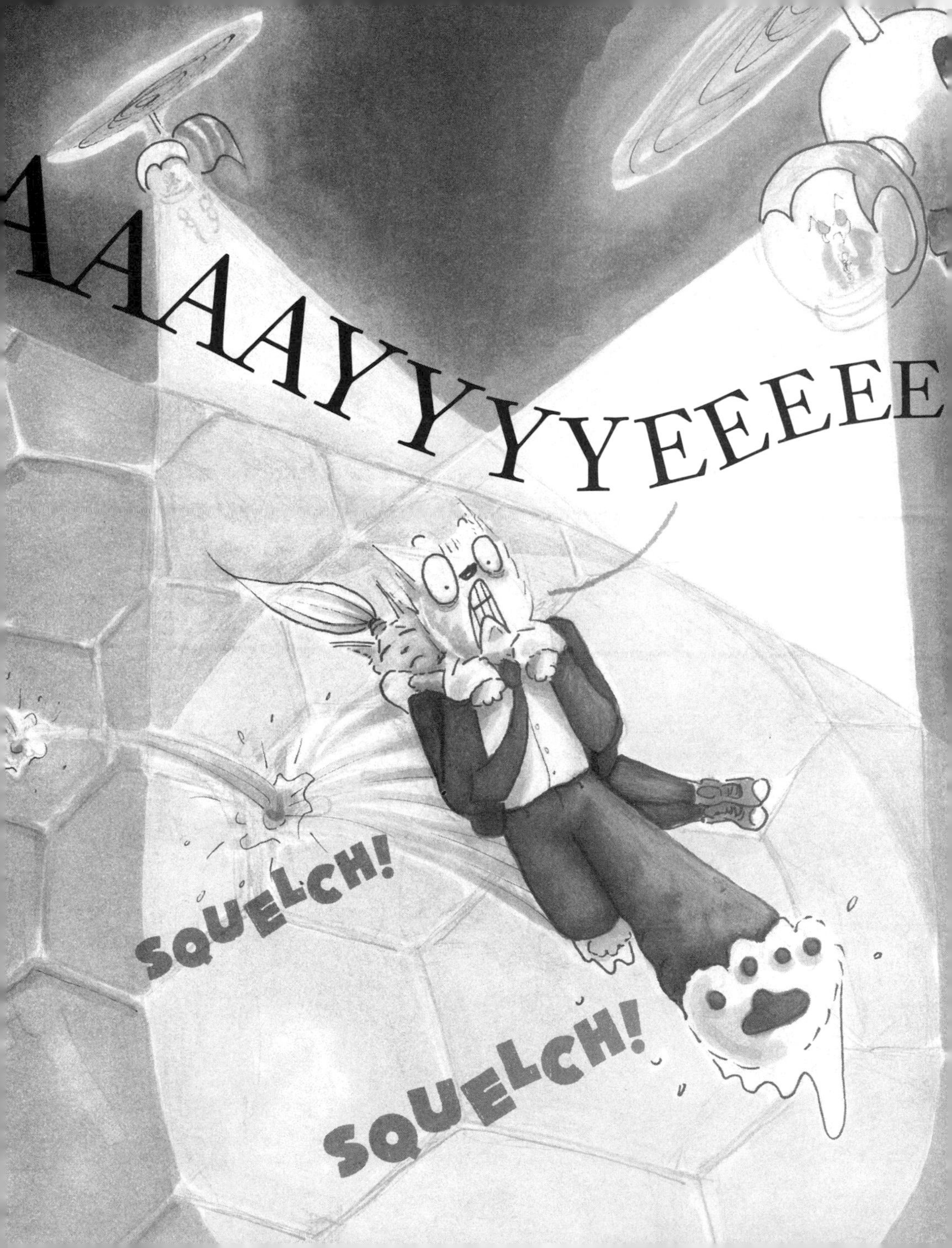
AAAAYYYYEEEEE
SQUELCH!
SQUELCH!

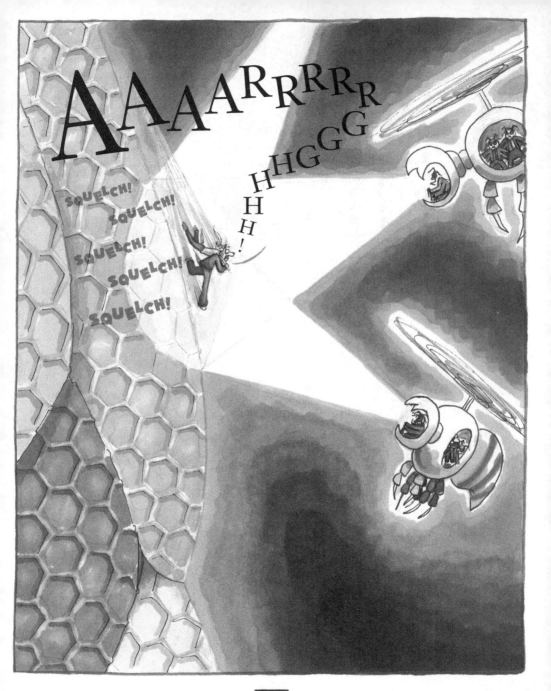

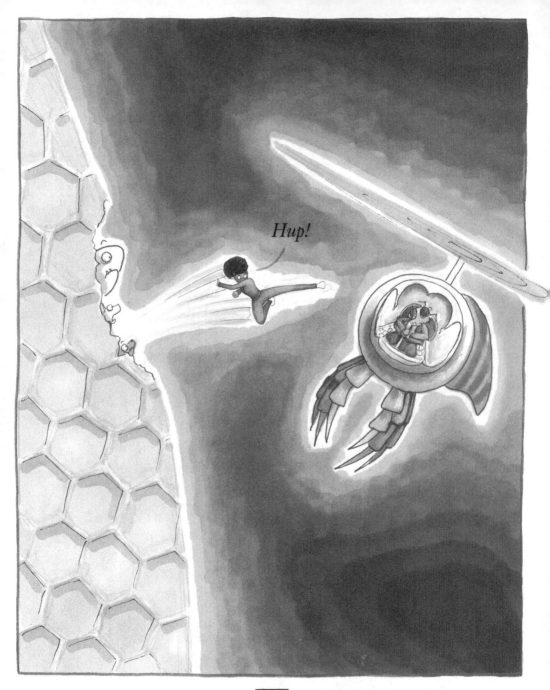

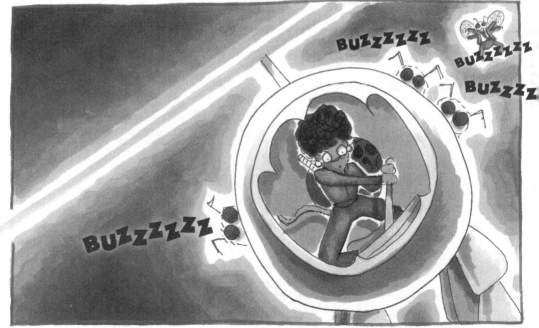

BUZZZZZZZ
BUZZZZZZZ
BUZZZZZZZ
SQUELCH!
SQUELCH!
THIS WAS A TERRIBLE IDEA!
ELCH!
SQUELCH!

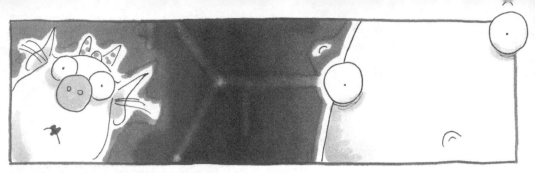

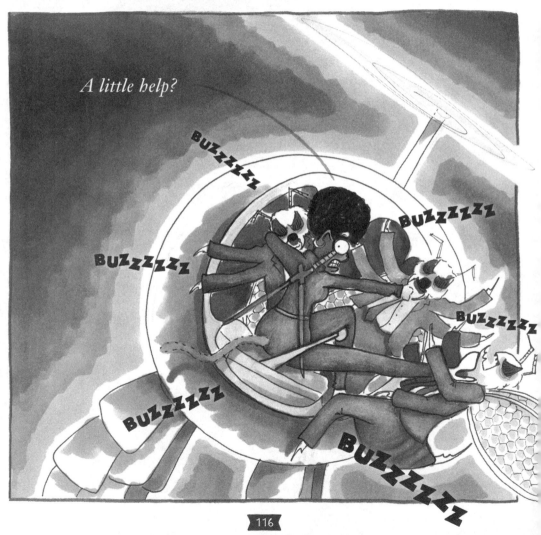

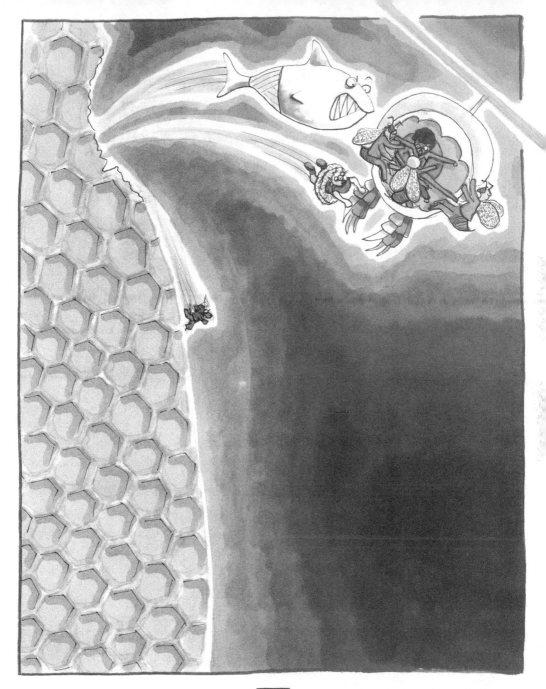

# LET'S GO SAVE
# PIRANHA.

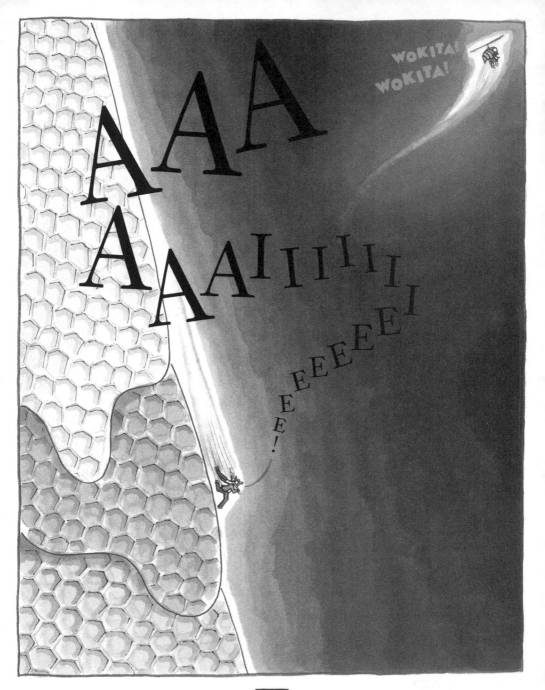

Wolfie?

*HEEEEEY!*
YOU'RE AWAKE!

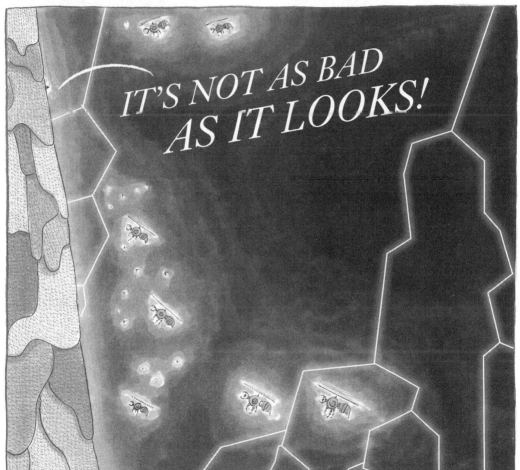

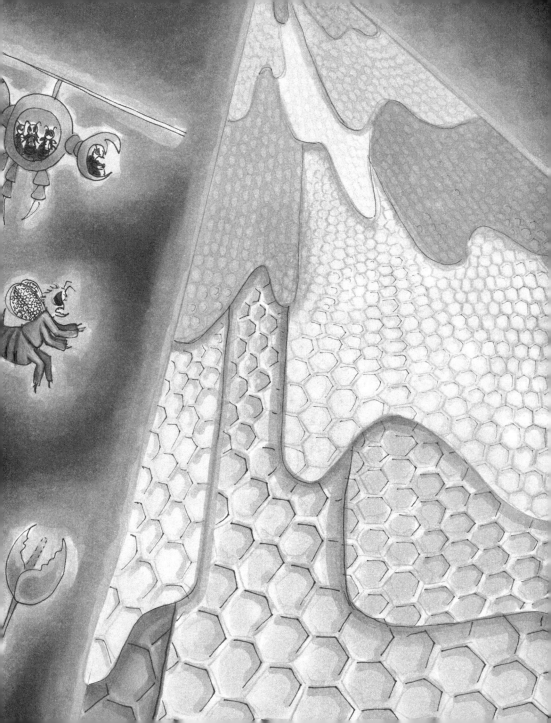

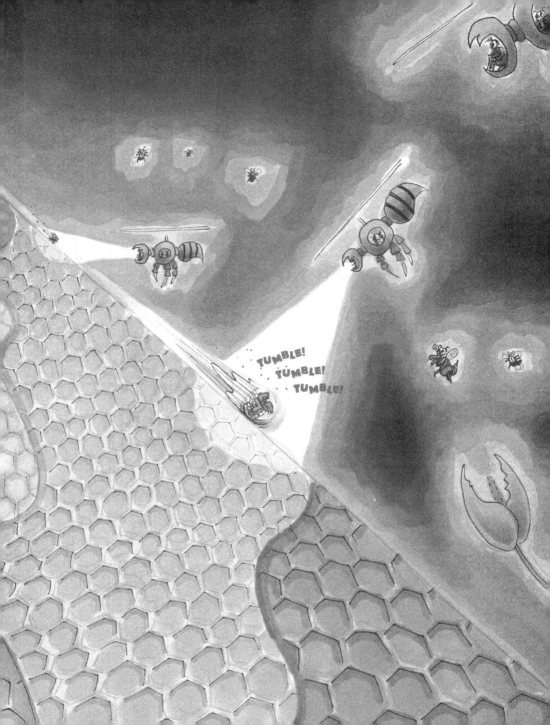

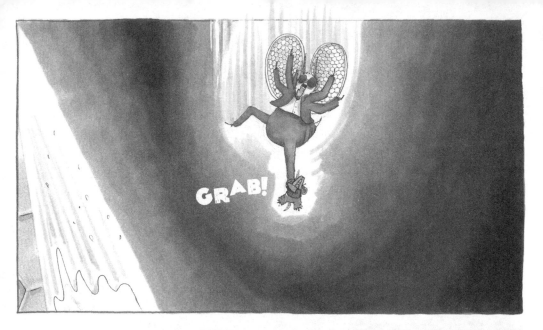

SPLAT!

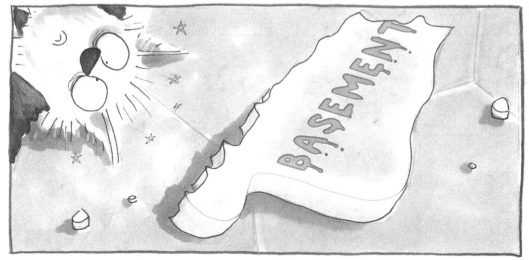

# · CHAPTER 7 ·
# WHO'S IN CHARGE HERE?!

*Do it*, Boof.

Or whatever your name is . . .

His *name* is BUCK!

# BUCK THUNDERS!

And he at least **LOOKS** like he knows what he's doing. We should listen to Buck!

I can't believe I'm saying this, but the spider is right.

## STOP THE SHIP!

STOP THE SHIP, PLEASE.

NO WAY!
I . . . wha . . . HEY!
Oooh . . . You know what?!
**I SUDDENLY FEEL LIKE STOPPING THE SHIP!**
So . . . YEAH!
**I WILL!**

PHRRT!

WAIT!

*WHY DID I JUST STOP THE SHIP?!*

**BECAUSE IT'S THE RIGHT THING TO DO.**

**CAN YOU FEEL IT?**

*I can.*
*I really can . . .*

*Weird.*
*Yes.*
*I can feel it, too.*

I'M HAVING TROUBLE BREATHING, AND I DON'T KNOW WHAT TO FEEL!

I kinda *feel* like my leadership is being undermined, but I'm **AWESOME** enough to be cool with that.

*WHY ARE YOU EVEN HERE?!*

**PUT ALL OUR POWER INTO THE TRACTOR BEAM.**

*WHAT?!*

YOU WANT TO TRAP IT IN THE TRACTOR BEAM?!

**YOU WANT TO CAPTURE IT?!**

WHAT WILL YOU DO WITH IT ONCE YOU'VE GOT IT?!

YOU DON'T NEED TO WORRY ABOUT THAT.

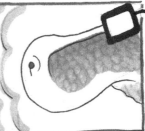

HEY, CHIEF! *I'M* THE LEADER OF THIS MISSION!

*SAYS WHO?!*

*SAYS* **BUCK!**

# TIFFANY!

Why are you defending this

## TOTAL RANDOM?!

*WHO CARES WHAT HE THINKS?!*

Well, *that* explains a lot . . .

Milton!

The TRACTOR BEAM is at full power . . .
**READY TO FIRE.**

**FIRE IT, NATHAN.**

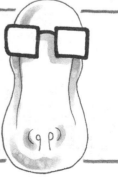

# · CHAPTER 8 ·
# THE BASEMENT

Yeah.
Long story.

Do you think one of these is
**THE DOORWAY?**

I guess so.

You sure the **HEAVY-METAL CENTIPEDE** isn't here?

I'm sure.

He's **HIDING** beyond all these doorways, waiting.

He won't strike until our team gets **WEAKENED** and thinned out by his **EVIL FLUNKIES,** and I'm left . . .

You won't get rid
of me that easily!

ARGH!

Oh, I do love him.

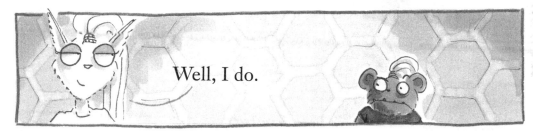

Well, I do.

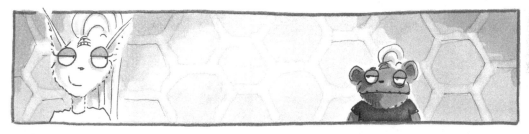

And he found **THE DOORWAY!**

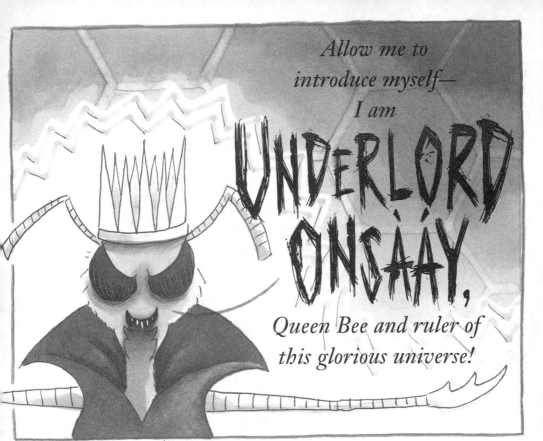

Allow me to introduce myself—
I am

# UNDERLORD ONSÀÁY,

*Queen Bee and ruler of this glorious universe!*

You're . . . Queen Bee Onsàáy?

Yes . . .

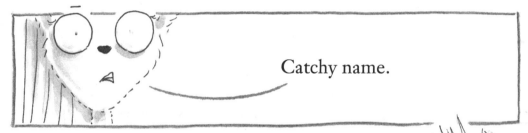

Catchy name.

*Well, aren't you* **CHARMING.**
*One question, though, darling—*
*what made you think you're*
*a match for . . .*

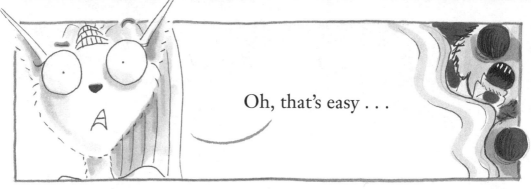

Oh, that's easy . . .

I'm
THE ONE.

*Hurgh!*

FLIP!

Well, *that* was easy.

# · CHAPTER 9 ·
# THE V.I.P.

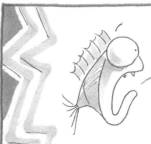

Mr. Snake!
*What are you doing, man?!*
**WE LOVE YOU!**
Just come home and . . .

FEEL MY POWER, PIRANHA. GIVE IN TO IT.

NO CAN DO!

*YOU CAN'T USE YOUR WITCHY POWERS ON ME!*

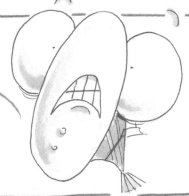

I *literally* don't understand a word you're saying!

# DON'T PLAY GAMES WITH ME!
And don't misuse "literally," either.

Seriously, bro!
I don't know what you mean!
Sure, they've started calling me

**THE ORACLE,**

but I can't figure out why.
I was hoping you could tell *me!*

The Oracle?

YEAH, that's right!

I'm THE ORACLE, homie!

I'm like a V.I.P.

## VERY. IMPORTANT. PIRANHA.

So, you'd better let me go, you know what I'm sayin'?

It's only a matter of time before the gang turns up here trying to rescue me, you *know?*

Oh, I know.

In fact, I'm COUNTING ON IT.

# · CHAPTER 10 ·
# OPEN WIDE!

Wolfie?

Shortfuse?

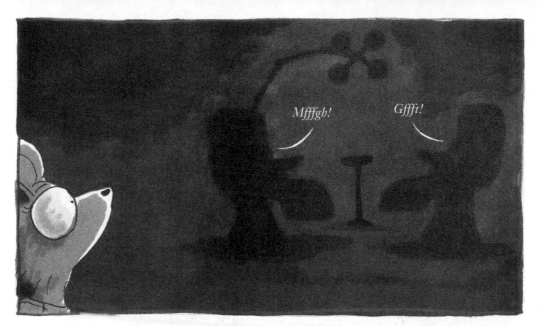

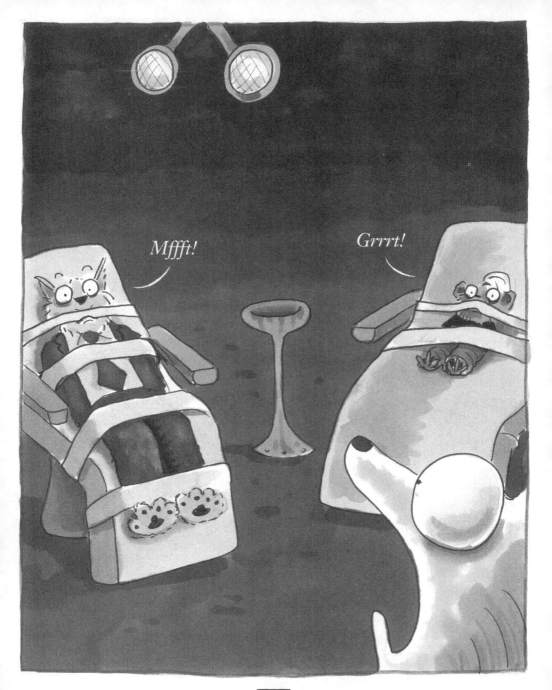

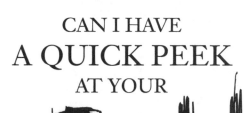

TO BE CONTINUED . . .

# *REMINDER!*

You have a checkup scheduled at the:

DRILLAÄRGH HOSPITAL OF EXPERIMENTAL DENTISTRY.

Please don't eat or drink anything 12 hours prior to your appointment. Make sure to wear comfortable shoes, as running away from our highly unqualified dental staff can be tiring for some patients.

We look forward to seeing you!

Your appointment time is:

the BAD GUYS BOOK
COMING SOON!